This book belongs to:

_____

_____

_____

First published 2000 by Walker Books Ltd
87 Vauxhall Walk, London SE1 1 5HJ

4 6 8 10 9 7 5

© 2000 Lucy Cousins
Lucy Cousins font © 2000 Lucy Cousins

Based on the Audio Visual Series "Maisy". A King Rollo Films Production for
Universal Pictures Visual Programming. Original Script by Andrew Brenner.

Printed in China

British Library Cataloguing in Publication Data:
a catalogue record for this book is
available from the British Library

0-7445-7277-0

Maisy's Bathtime

Lucy Cousins

WALKER BOOKS
AND SUBSIDIARIES
LONDON • BOSTON • SYDNEY

It's Maisy's bathtime.

She runs the water and puts in some bubbles ...

and in goes Duck.

Ding-dong!
Oh, that's
the doorbell.

Maisy runs downstairs to see who it is.

Hello, Tallulah.

Maisy can't play now, it's her bathtime.

Maisy runs back upstairs and gets undressed.

Maisy jumps in the bubbly bath.

Ding-dong!
Who is ringing the doorbell now?

It's Tallulah again.
Maisy's having
her bath now.
Come and play
later, Tallulah.

Oh! Where are you going, Tallulah?

Tallulah goes to
the bathroom
and takes off
her clothes.

Splash, splash!

Maisy and Tallulah
play in the bath.

Hooray!

If you're crazy for Maisy, you'll love these books featuring Maisy and her friends.

  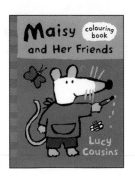 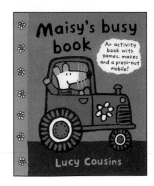

Other titles

Maisy's ABC • Maisy Goes to Bed • Maisy Goes to the Playground
Maisy Goes Swimming • Maisy Goes to Playschool
Maisy's House • Happy Birthday, Maisy • Maisy at the Farm